W9-AFC-128

Robin
and the Friar
and
the

Tales of Robin Hood

HOWARD COUNTY LIBRARY
BIG SPRING, TEXAS

This edition first published in 2009
by Sea-to-Sea Publications
Distributed by Black Rabbit Books
P.O. Box 3263
Mankato, Minnesota 56002

Text © Damian Harvey 2006, 2009
Illustration © Martin Remphry 2006

Printed in China

All rights reserved

A CIP catalog record for this book is
available from the Library of Congress.

ISBN 978-1-59771-177-7

9 8 7 6 5 4 3 2 1

Published by arrangement with the
Watts Publishing Group Ltd, London.

Series Editor: Jackie Hamley
Series Advisors: Dr. Linda Gambrell, Dr. Barrie Wade
Series Designer: Peter Scoulding

Robin

and the Friar

by Damian Harvey and Martin Remphry

SEA-TO-SEA

Mankato Collingwood London

Sherwood Forest was filled with the clang of swords and the thud of arrows hitting their targets.

Robin Hood and his merry men were enjoying the summer's day.

Will Scarlet, Much the Miller's son, and Little John were practicing with their bows.

"I'm proud to have the best archers in the land," said Robin Hood.

7

But Will Scarlet laughed. "I hear there's a friar at Fountains Abbey who could beat us all!" he said.

"Then I'll not rest until I meet this friar!" cried Robin Hood.

Robin put on his chainmail shirt,
picked up his sword and bow, then
set off for Fountains Abbey.

As Robin walked, he came across a friar eating his lunch by the river.

"If you were a good man," said
Robin Hood, "you'd carry me
across this river."

The friar saw Robin's sword
and bow, and agreed to carry
him across.

When they reached the other side,
Robin Hood jumped to the ground.
Then the friar drew his sword.

"Now," said the friar, "you carry
me back so I can finish my lunch."
The friar's sword looked sharp,
so Robin agreed.

The water was cold and Robin
slipped and slithered on the stones.

At last they reached the other side and the friar jumped to the ground. The friar was about to finish his lunch when Robin drew his sword.

"Now," said Robin, "carry me
back or you will feel the point
of my sword."

Robin climbed onto the friar's
shoulders and off they went.

But this time, the friar threw Robin into the water! "I hope you can swim," laughed the friar.

Robin Hood kicked and splashed
to the side of the river.

Then he drew his bow. "I'm going to pin your robes to that tree!" shouted Robin.

He took aim and fired an arrow,
but the friar turned it away with
his shield.

"Is that the best you can do?"
laughed the friar.

Robin fired another arrow.
But again the friar turned it
away. Robin fired until all
his arrows had gone.

"Now, draw your sword, friar!" yelled Robin. Robin and the friar fought all day, but neither one could beat the other.

"That's enough!" cried Robin Hood. "You must be the friar of Fountains Abbey. I came looking for you!

"If you join me and my merry men in Sherwood Forest you'll have all the food you can eat and a new robe."

The friar looked at his tattered robe and nodded. "No man has stood against me before," he said. "I'll happily join you."

From that point on, Robin Hood and Friar Tuck became the best of friends.

If you enjoyed this story, why not try another one?

There are 12 Hopscotch Adventures to choose from:

TALES OF KING ARTHUR

1. The Sword in the Stone
ISBN 978-1-59771-176-0

2. Arthur the King
ISBN 978-1-59771-173-9

3. The Round Table
ISBN 978-1-59771-175-3

4. Sir Lancelot and the Ice Castle
ISBN 978-1-59771-174-6

TALES OF ROBIN HOOD

Robin and the Knight
ISBN 978-1-59771-178-4

Robin and the Monk
ISBN 978-1-59771-179-1

Robin and the Friar
ISBN 978-1-59771-177-7

Robin and the Silver Arrow
ISBN 978-1-59771-180-7

MORE ADVENTURES

Aladdin and the Lamp
ISBN 978-1-59771-181-4

Blackbeard the Pirate
ISBN 978-1-59771-182-1

George and the Dragon
ISBN 978-1-59771-183-8

Jack the Giant-Killer
ISBN 978-1-59771-184-5